**Today Bob is going to pl[ay]
games with his No.1 Van.
It has lots of special features.**

Roof rack
with ties

Loud hooter

Go-fast
button

Easy-open
back doors

Bob's
No.1
Van

Extra-
strong
bumper

Quick-release
back wheels

Escape door
with handle

Extra-slip
tyres

Loud Hooting

Here is Bob sitting in his No. 1 Van.
Bob loves to do loud hooting. He can do
loud hoots and very, very loud hoots!

Go, Bob, Go!

Bob is giving Mr Thornton-Jones and friends
a lift. Bob likes singing as he drives along.

"La de dum dum de dah!"

Pack and Crash

This is one of Bob's favourite games.
Bob packs his No.1 Van with lots of things.

Bob's
No.1
Van

○ ○ ○ ○ ○
Chair
Sticks
Socks
cushions
water
books
duvet
Scarf
teddy
lunchbox

Bob's friend **Giorgio** is going to play
Pack and **Crash** with **Bob**. Here he is
packing his **Mini Dot Trailer Car** with
buckets full of paint.

purple paint
blue paint
red paint
yellow paint
grey paint
orange paint
black paint
white paint
pink paint
green paint

Now look at Bob. He is driving really fast.

And Giorgio is driving really fast.

Snack Time

Bob likes sitting on his No. 1 Van and eating his packed lunch. Today he has one apple,

Munch! Munch!

one banana milkshake,

Slurp! Slurp!

and one very noisy packet of crisps.

Bumper Bash

Bob is getting ready to play Bumper Bash with his friends.

Clemence has lots of bouncy balls in the back of his car.

Vroom! Vroom!

Tate has packed his big suitcase.

Vroom! Vroom!

**Vroom!
Vroom!**

Jo-Jo and the Triplets
have tied a cushion
to the Beetle Car.

**Vroom!
Vroom!**

Bob is revving up
the engine of his
No.1 Van.

Ready, steady ...

Bumper Bash!
"Look at Jo-Jo's boots go!"
"Bash! Got you, Tate!"
Boing!
Bump!

Bye-bye, Bob

It is getting late now. Bob has played some great games with his No.1 Van and now he is tired. He has put his bed up on his roof rack and here he is having a little snooze.